CHRISTMAS
IN NEW MEXICO

Sue Carabine

Illustrations by
Shauna Mooney Kawasaki

Gibbs Smith, Publisher

First Edition
09 08 07   5 4 3 2

Text and illustrations © 2003
by Gibbs Smith, Publisher

Published by
Gibbs Smith, Publisher
P.O. Box 667
Layton, Utah 84041

Orders: 1-800-748-5439
www.gibbs-smith.com

Edited by Linda Nimori
Designed and produced by Mary Ellen Thompson,
    TTA Design
Printed and bound in China

ISBN10: 1-58685-273-6
ISBN13: 978-1-58685-273-3

'Twas the night before Christmas
in New Mexico,
The reindeer and Santa
were ready to go.

The Land of Enchantment
was tops on their list;
At this beautiful season,
there's no place like this.

Santa was more than
excited this year,
His jubilant sparkle
rubbed off on his deer.

THE LAND OF ENCHANTMENT

As Mrs. Claus waved,
bade them all fond farewell,
She whispered, "Remember
the young girl from Roswell."

Nick knew whom she meant.
It was part of the reason
That he was so joyful
this holiday season.

A sweet little girl
had written a letter
That Nick, after reading,
said, "It's time I met her!

"Dear Santa,"
the cute little letter began,
"I need something for Grandpa,
a wonderful man.

THE LAND OF ENCHANTMENT

"Though I live with my mom,
he takes good care of us,
Whatever we ask him,
he ne'er makes a fuss.

"He looks just like you, Nick,
with a snowy white beard,
So I'm asking your help
as this Christmas draws near.

"I'll give him a present,
a most precious gift,
Please help me to choose it;
you'll know what to pick."

Now, that's why St. Nick
and his deer flew so fast
O'er the caverns at Carlsbad
to Roswell, at last.

They picked up sweet Mary
who grinned with delight,
She cried, "Thank you, Nick!"
Then the huge sleigh took flight.

Albuquerque, their first stop,
was sparkling below.
Said Mary, "We'll find
something here, Nick, I know."

"It shouldn't be hard,"
Nick said, "I have found
There are wonderful things
in this city, year round."

"Would your grandpa enjoy
riding in a balloon?
A fiesta is held here
each autumn—it's cool."

"Oh, Santa, I'd love that,
but my dear old grandpa
Would much rather travel
by horse or by car!"

Then Nick showed sweet Mary
his collegiate picks
As the sleigh hovered over
old Route 66:

"New Mexico offers
two really great schools,
Down there—UNM,
also NMSU!"

They swooped into Old Town
to a western boutique,
Donning chaps, boots, and Stetson,
Nick really looked chic!

"That looks just great, Nick,
but my grandpa, I fear,
Wears a hat he's been wearing
for the past fifty years!"

Climbing back in the sleigh,
Nick called, "Hold on tight!
Santa Fe's coming up
and you're in for a sight.

Luminarias lined driveways
and sidewalks of homes;
They sparkled on rooftops
and adobe-style domes.

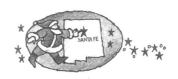

"I love this place, Santa,
everything is so pretty!"
"It's Christmastime, dear,
in the capital city!

"Let's choose for your grandpa
art, jewelry, or weavings."
"But, Nick, his life's simple;
they'd have little meaning."

Hearing peals in the distance
from sonorous bells,
They walked down the old streets,
followed wonderful smells.

"Does Grandpa like chiles,
posole, fajitas?
Or maybe tamales,
enchiladas, burritos?"

"Oh, yes, he does, Nick,
but often he tells me,
'No food is like Grandma's,
and it never will be!

Then, Santa Claus grinned,
'cause he quite understood,
Told her, "As you can tell,
Mrs. Claus makes food GOOD!

THE LAND OF ENCHANTMENT

"Now, there're places to visit
before we must leave,
The Palace of the Governors
you surely must see.

"And following that
a museum so rare,
The artwork of Georgia
O'Keeffe is found there!"

They both felt inspired
(what wonderful places!),
And left with expressions
of awe on their faces.

Then farther up north,
Santa guided the sleigh,
To a most charming village.
'Twas right on their way.

Flying over Chimayo,
Nick whispered, "Young lass,
let's pause for a while here
to listen to Mass."

La Chuchilla was filled with
good folks Christmas Eve,
Giving thanks for sweet Jesus,
in whom they believed.

For a moment they listened:
soft strains filled the air
In Spanish and English—
carols sung with great care.

"And, now, Las Posadas!"
Nick turned Mary 'round
And both went to join in
the procession downtown.

They browsed outdoor markets,
saw ristras so red
and Yule decorations.
"This is fun!" Mary said.

They talked with the Navajo,
Zuni, Apache, and Ute.
Soon, both were delighted
they'd traveled this route.

THE LAND OF ENCHANTMENT

In Taos, Swift Eagle
taught Native traditions
To children who all had
bright hopes and ambitions.

"There's great skiing here,"
cried Nick. "Let's take time,
Get passes for Grandpa—
he's right in his prime!"

St. Nick's eyes were twinkling
as he uttered these words.
She laughed, "Gramps would say,
'Now, that's strictly for birds!'"

Asked Nick, "How 'bout rafting?"

when they crossed Rio Grande.

Mary said, "Grandpa keeps

both his feet on the ground!"

Their journey now over,
Nick heard Mary sigh,
"I guess I'll give Grandpa
some socks that I'll buy."

"If I were your grandpa,
I'd feel ten feet tall
If I knew that you loved me
the best of them all!"

Then Mary paused, smiling,
"Thanks, Nick, I feel better,"
And promptly sat down
to write Grandpa a letter.

THE LAND OF ENCHANTMENT

"Dear Grandpa, I've searched
for the right Christmas gift
All over this state—
even dwellings in cliffs!"

"From Las Cruces to Shiprock
and Las Vegas to Hobbs,
Sharing Christmas with you folks
is my most favorite job!"

As Santa prepared
to leave New Mexico,
He gazed on it fondly,
said, "I hate to go."

THE LAND OF ENCHANTMENT

"We soared over mountains
and rivers so blue,
But this Christmas I want you
to know I love you!"